推薦序 Foreword

辜仲諒
中國信託慈善基金會董事長

　　作者顏維萱Valerie Yen是我的表姪女，自小面對家中長輩因疾病而產生遺忘、離別的議題，有所反思，這本書就是Valerie想和大家分享的內容，在我反覆閱讀繪本的時候，彷彿感受到親人的溫暖依舊伴我身旁，這也許就是生命存在的價值與意義。

　　我們都渴望生命停留在高處，實際上生命是起起伏伏、是一次又一次的告別和新的開展，Valerie年紀雖小，卻有如此深刻、細膩的體悟，以純真清新的畫風筆觸勾勒故事，這本繪本值得讀者細細品味，邀請大朋友小朋友翻開書本來一趟心靈旅程，相信只要我們帶上回憶中的每一份美好能量，就能有十足勇氣面對下一個挑戰，綻放更多生命中的花火。

Mama!

I don't want to leave!

"Mama, I don't want to move away!"
Baby Wind cried.

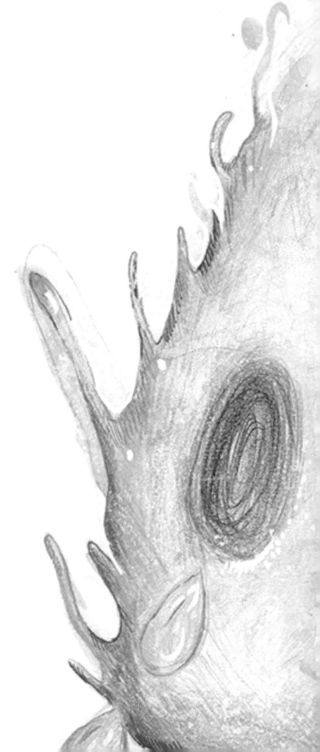

"Why is that?" Mama Wind gently asked, "Don't we always move to new places after a while?"

Because... because I'm afraid Lili will forget about me.

We've always been inseparable, traveling to so many places together.
I'm afraid once I leave, she won't remember me anymore.

Mama Wind: How could that be?

No matter where you go,

Or how far you travel,

Even if you can't be together at every moment,

She will not forget you.

Lili will be able to
hear your whispers
in the wind

See you in the dances
of dandelions.

14

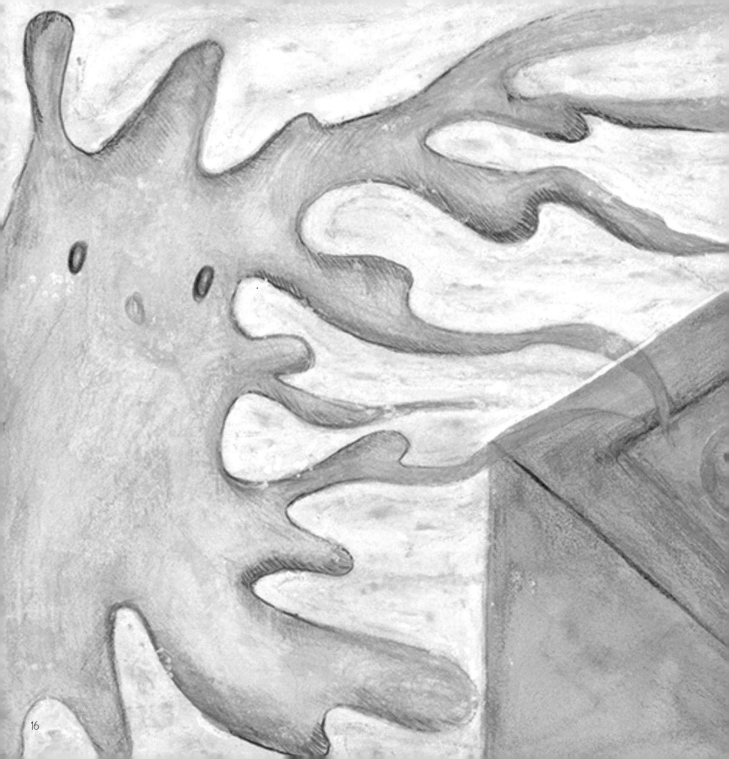

Capture a hint of you in the smell of freshly baked cookies from the oven

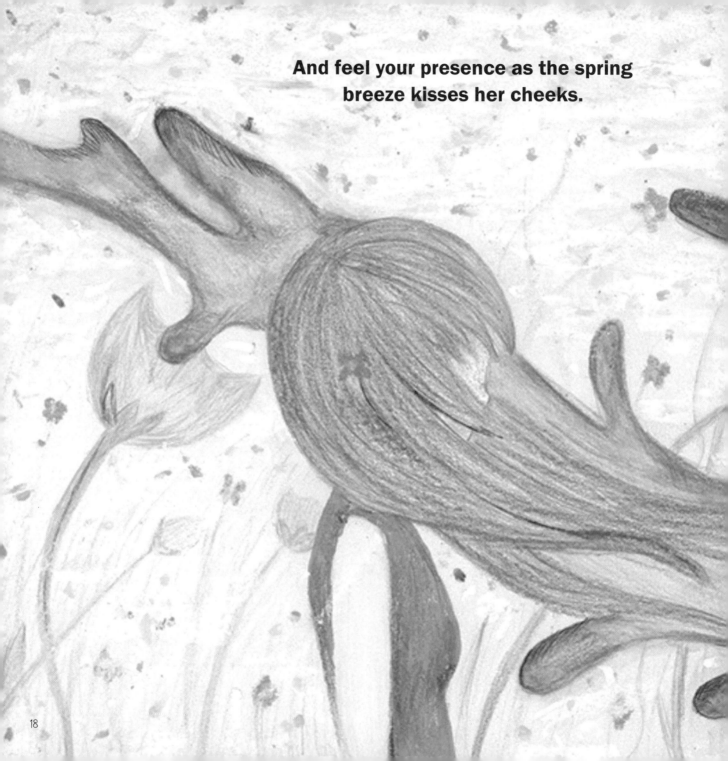

And feel your presence as the spring breeze kisses her cheeks.

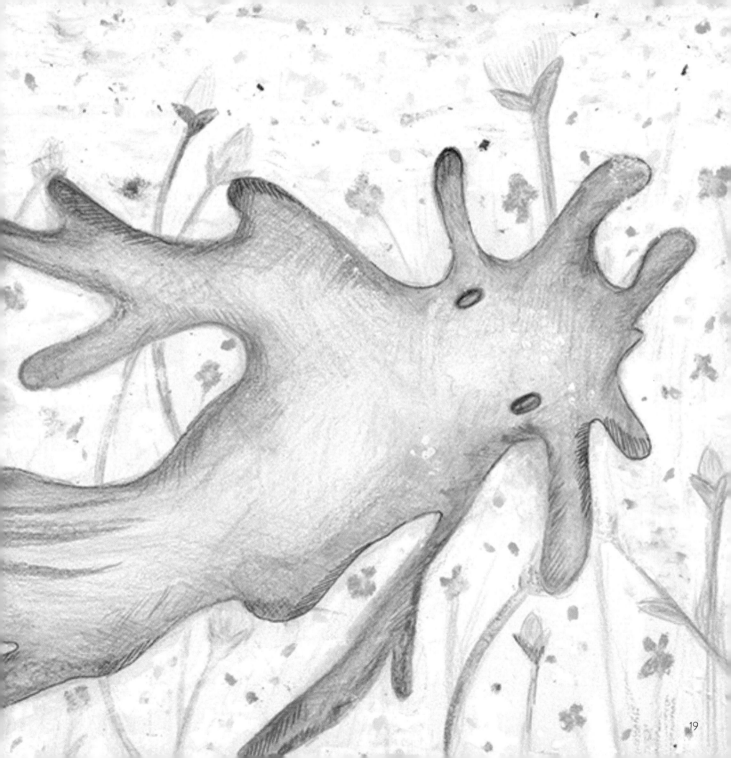

She'll hold you in her heart, unforgotten, forevermore.

You will always car

22

piece of each other.

With Mama Wind's soft whisper, Baby Wind smiled, his heart filled with beautiful memories of Lili.

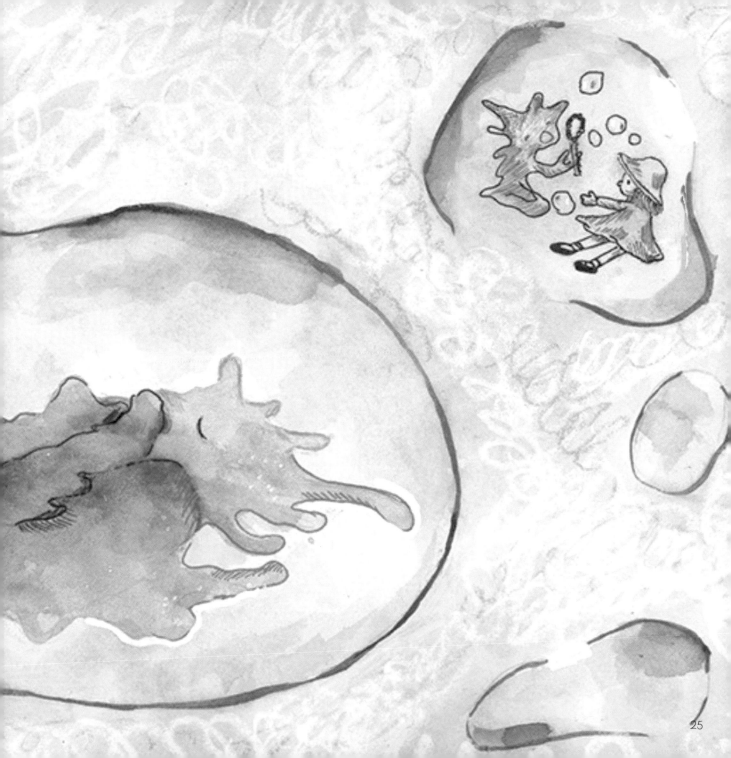

About the Author

Valerie Yen

11th-grade student at Taipei American School
Founder of To the Moon Art Charity

About the Association

To the Moon Art Charity is a student-run nonprofit organization that empowers individuals aged 15 to 35 to engage in diverse philanthropic initiatives. Our mission is to use art as a tool to support vulnerable groups, promote quality education, and preserve cultural and historical heritage.

We are dedicated to promoting educational innovation, cultural preservation, and social inclusion through creative expression. Through the positive impact of art, we aspire to advance the overall welfare of society and create a more vibrant and inclusive world for all.

About the Book

Inspired by the cognitive issues and other illnesses affecting many of her elderly family members, Valerie began to think deeply about life. Through this picture book, she explores touching questions:

How can we say a sincere goodbye even if we can never meet again? Does separation mean forgetting? Does disappearing mean ceasing to exist?

In exploring these deep and challenging questions, Valerie uses the wind to represent emotions and memories that we can feel but not see. She also uses the story of the wind baby moving to symbolize saying goodbye.

Mama! I don't want to leave!

作　　者　Valerie Yen
發 行 人　孫珮頤
出　　版　登月藝術慈善組織
　　　　　105台北市松山區光復南路67號11樓
　　　　　電話：（02）2747-5670
　　　　　傳眞：（02）2747-4310
設計編印　白象文化事業有限公司
　　　　　專案主編：李婕　經紀人：徐錦淳
經銷代理　白象文化事業有限公司
　　　　　412台中市大里區科技路1號8樓之2（台中軟體園區）
　　　　　出版專線：（04）2496-5995　　傳眞：（04）2496-9901
　　　　　401台中市東區和平街228巷44號（經銷部）
　　　　　購書專線：（04）2220-8589　　傳眞：（04）2220-8505
印　　刷　基盛印刷工場
初版一刷　2024年8月
I S B N　978-626-98608-1-4
定　　價　320元